Anthony Browne

WILLY THE WIMP

Alfred A. Knopf · New York

THIS IS A BORZOI BOOK PUBLISHED BY ALFRED A. KNOPF, INC.

Copyright © 1984 by Anthony Browne
All rights reserved under International and Pan-American Copyright Conventions.
Published in the United States by Alfred A. Knopf, Inc., New York,
and simultaneously in Canada by Random House of Canada Limited, Toronto.
Distributed by Random House, Inc., New York.
Originally published by Julia MacRae Books in Great Britain.
Manufactured in Belgium   First American Edition
2   4   6   8   10   9   7   5   3   1

Library of Congress Cataloging in Publication Data
Browne, Anthony.   Willy the wimp.
Summary: A young chimpanzee, tired of being bullied by the suburban
gorilla gang, decides to build up his muscles so he won't be a wimp anymore.
1. Children's stories, English.   [1. Chimpanzees—Fiction.
2. Bodybuilding—Fiction.   3. Bullies—Fiction]   I. Title.
PZ7.B81984Wi   1985   [E]   84–14320
ISBN 0–394–87061–1   ISBN 0–394–97061–6 (lib. bdg.)

For Joseph

Willy wouldn't hurt a fly.

Willy worried about stepping on
tiny insects every time he went
for a walk. When someone knocked
into him, he always said,
"Oh, I'm sorry!"
Even when it wasn't his fault.

Sometimes when he was out walking,
the suburban gorilla gang bullied him.
"Oh, I'm sorry!" said Willy
when they hit him.
The suburban gorillas called him
Willy the Wimp.

Willy hated that name. Willy the Wimp!

One evening when Willy was reading his comic book, he saw . . .

DONT BE A *WIMP!*

I <u>was</u> a scrawny, skinny-chested
pathetic weakling. NOW........
I can order people about..........
kick sand in THEIR faces...
talk VERY LOUDLY.....
lift heavy things......
get R-E-S-P-E-C-T.
Do YOU want.........
Bulging arm muscles..
Tireless legs..........
A deep chest...........
A large wardrobe...........
A magnetic personality?
MAIL THIS *NOW!*

That sounds like just the thing for me,
thought Willy. So he sent some money to
the address in the advertisement.

He rushed to the door every morning
to catch the postman. "Oh, I'm sorry!"
said Willy when the postman brought
nothing for him.

But one day a package arrived . . .

This was it! Willy opened it excitedly.
Inside was a book: it told Willy
what to do . . .

First some exercises.

Then some jogging.

Willy had to go on a special diet.

He went to aerobics classes
where everybody danced to
disco music. Willy felt a bit silly.

He learned how to box.

And he went to a body-building club.

Willy took up weight lifting, and gradually over
weeks and months Willy got bigger . . . and bigger . . .

Willy looked in the mirror.
He liked what he saw.

So when Willy walked down the street

and saw the suburban gorillas attacking Millie . . .

They ran.

"Oh . . . Willy," said Millie.

"What, Millie?" said Willy.

"You're my hero, Willy," said Millie.

"Oh . . . Millie," said Willy.

Willy was proud.

"I'm not a wimp!"

I'm a hero!

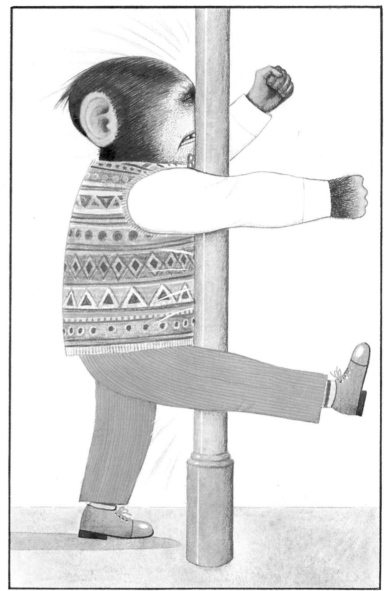

BANG!

"Oh, I'm sorry!" said Willy.